Teeny Tiny Ernest

Ernest Series™

Teeny Tiny Ernest is part of the Ernest Series.

Barnesyard Books and Ernest are trademarks of Barnesyard Books, Inc.

Book design by Christine Wolstenholme

Published by Barnesyard Books, Sergeantsville, NJ 08557
www.barnesyardbooks.com

Printed in China

Library of Congress Catalog Card Number: 00-91896

ISBN 0-9674681-1-6

Teeny Tiny Ernest

by Laura T. Barnes

Illustrated by Carol A. Camburn

to Amy —
always remember
the love of animals.
Carol A. Camburn
October 1, 2000

To Amy,
It's what's
in your heart
that makes
you special!
Laura T. Barnes
+ Ernest 😊

BARNESYARD BOOKS™

Sergeantsville, NJ 08557 • www.barnesyardbooks.com

For Ernest – my spunky little guy.

– L.T.B.

For Billy – my inspiration, my gift.

– C.A.C.

Ernest is a miniature donkey. A teeny, tiny, little donkey – much, much smaller than other donkeys.

Ernest didn't like being so small.
He kept waiting for the day that he would grow to be big and tall. But he never did.

Everywhere he looked it seemed that everyone was taller than he was.

The other donkeys were bigger.

The cows were bigger.

And the horse was much, much bigger.

Even the newborn horse was bigger than Ernest.

The frisky colt had very long legs that made him taller than the little donkey.
Ernest couldn't believe that even the baby horse was bigger than he was.

Ernest spent his days in the pasture looking at the other animals.

"Why can't I be big like they are?" wondered Ernest.

Ernest tried to do whatever he could to make himself look taller.

He climbed to the top of the dirt pile and pretended to eat grass. He was sure that he looked much taller when he stood on top of the little hill.

When the cows walked by he raised his head as high as he could and smiled. "Hee haw. Hee haw," said Ernest trying to get their attention.

"What on earth is he doing?" said the cows giggling.
They didn't know why Ernest was standing on the hill.
They just smiled and kept on walking.

Ernest climbed down from the little hill. His plan did not work.
"The cows didn't even notice that I looked taller," thought Ernest.

Ernest slowly walked back to the stable. "Why can't I be big like them?" he wondered.

As Ernest got closer to the stable he saw Travis, the horse, eating grass.

Ernest got an idea. "I know how I can look bigger," he said.

He quickly climbed up the ramp into the stable. When he got to the top of the ramp, he turned around and acted like he was looking out over the pasture. He stretched his ears and neck up as high as he could. He was trying to look as tall as possible.

When Travis saw Ernest, he walked over. "Hi Ernest," said Travis fondly. "What are you looking at?"

Ernest was so busy stretching that he didn't even hear him.

He stretched and stretched. It was no use. Travis still towered over Ernest.

"Is something the matter?" asked Travis.

"No, nothing," muttered Ernest. He stopped stretching and put his head down.
Sadly he walked slowly back down the ramp.

"Something is the matter," said Travis.
He could see that Ernest was sad.
"What is it Ernest?"

"I'm tired of being so tiny," explained Ernest.
"I'm the tiniest animal in the pasture."

"Hmmm," thought Travis. He then looked out at the
pasture. He saw the other donkeys, cows and horses. "Well yes,
I guess you are smaller," he remarked. "I never noticed before."

"You never noticed before?" asked a shocked Ernest. "How could you not notice?"

"I just didn't," explained Travis.

"How could you not notice how tiny I am?" Ernest asked again.

The cows, who had been making their way up to the stable, heard part of the conversation. "What is all of this talk about being tiny?" asked the cow.

"I'm tired of being the tiniest animal in the pasture," repeated Ernest.

"Tiny?" questioned the cow. "Why yes, I guess you are little. I never thought about it before."

"You didn't notice either? How could you not notice?" asked Ernest.

"Well," added Travis, "you're our friend. You're nice, you're fun and you're funny! We like to spend our days with you in the pasture and eat in the stable with you at night."

"But, but you're all so much bigger than I am!" stuttered Ernest.

"Who cares if we're bigger? It makes no difference. No difference at all," said Travis. "Size doesn't matter. It's who you are that matters."

"Who I am is short!" shouted Ernest.

"No, no," said the cow. "You might be smaller than we are, but that's not really who you are.
That's only what you look like on the outside."

"Who you are comes from the inside," explained Travis. "It's how nice you are. It's what a good friend you are. It's how you treat others. And, most important of all, it's what's in your heart."

"Oh!" said Ernest. "I never thought of it that way."

"Plus, think of all the things that you can do that we can't," declared Travis.

"What can I do that you can't?" asked Ernest.

"Well," said Travis, "you can stand behind those bushes over there when it's cold and windy. Because of your size, you can stay warm and protected from the cold wind. I can't do that. I'm too big!"

"Yes, that's true," agreed Ernest. "I can do that."

"Remember when we play in the pasture and try to hide from each other?" asked the cow.

"Yes, I enjoy that," laughed Ernest. "That's fun!"

"It's fun for you," said the cow, "because you can hide behind that barrel. We can't do that. We're way too big. You always find us right away."

Ernest smiled and nodded, "I guess you're right. I never thought about it that way before."

"So you see," said Travis, "you can do many things that we can't. I think you're lucky."

"Lucky?" asked Ernest. He straightened up and suddenly felt very proud. "Yes, yes. Maybe I am. Yea for me!"

"You're a special friend with a big, big heart." reminded Travis. "You don't have to be tall to have a big heart!"

Ernest smiled. He realized that he was very special both inside and out.

He had a big, big heart and could do many things that the others couldn't.

"Hee haw. Hee haw," said Ernest. And he proudly trotted out into the pasture with all of his friends.